DOGGEREL

Canadian Cataloguing in Publication Data

Dalton, Sheila,
Doggerel

Poem.
ISBN 0-385-25533-0

1. Dogs – Juvenile poetry. 2. Children's poetry, Canadian (English).*
I. LaFave, Kim. II. Title.
PS8557.A4724D6 1996   jC811'.54   C95-933028-3

PZ8.3.D35Do 1996

Design by Roger Handling/Terra Firma Design
Printed and bound in the USA
Published in Canada by Doubleday Canada Limited,
105 Bond Street, Toronto, Ontario, Canada M5B 1Y3

For Gordon, who gave us Teddy.—S.D.

To Barb.—K.L.

DOGGEREL

Sheila Dalton • Illustrated by Kim LaFave

Doubleday Canada Limited

There are shaggy dogs, waggy dogs and dogs that have fleas

There are slow dogs and low dogs and dogs out on sprees

There are cute dogs and mute dogs that do without barks

There are mild dogs and wild dogs out making their marks

There are snappy dogs,
scrappy dogs
that just love a fight

Though ruthless,
if toothless,
they can't even bite

There are clown dogs and town dogs

Petite dogs,

and dogs that are squarish

elite dogs (some even quite rarish)

There are swell dogs, pell-mell dogs that race all around

And cheap dogs and sheepdogs and beagles and hounds

A Bassett's an asset
if you like your dogs droopy
But it's not cool, if they drool,

'cause they get you all goopy

There are bird dogs,
absurd dogs that point
on three legs

There are quick dogs
and trick dogs
that know how to beg

There are guard dogs, Bernard dogs that save mountaineers

There are scrawny dogs, yawny dogs and dogs with big ears

There are famous dogs, shamus dogs that help the police

There are howling dogs, prowling dogs
that chase after geese

There are flat dogs and fat dogs as jiggly as jelly

There are burly dogs,

curly dogs and

And poodles with oodles
of bows everywhere

dogs without hair

There are dumb dogs, though some dogs

There are working dogs, shirking dogs, dogs with big hearts

are smarter than smart

There are shedding dogs, sledding dogs (these have to be husky)

There are white dogs and light dogs and some that are dusky

There are young dogs, high-strung dogs

(they're usually yappy)

There are mad dogs and sad dogs—
though most seem quite happy

But the best, most-caressed dog
the one that's true blue
Is that neat dog, that sweet dog—
the one that loves you.